Violet
and the
Woof

Story by
Rebecca Grabill

Pictures by
Dasha Tolstikova

HARPER
An Imprint of HarperCollinsPublishers

ISBN 978-0-06-244110-2

The artist used ink wash, acrylic paint, pencils, and the computer to create the illustrations for this book.
Typography by Dana Fritts
18 19 20 21 22   SCP   10 9 8 7 6 5 4 3 2 1
❖
First Edition

To the Brave Explorers:
Penelope and Kilian
—R. G.

To my woof, Muffin!
—D. T.

"Once upon a time," Violet said, "a brave little girl and her brother set out on a long, *long* journey.

A journey fraught with danger and peril."

"The children had never traveled through
the woods all alone before," Violet said. "But
they were not scared."

"Until a fierce, ferocious wolf stopped them on the trail."

"WOOF!" said Peter.

"That's just a lady with her puppy,"
Violet said. "Not a wolf!"

"We're visiting our neighbor Papa Jean-Louis who lives beyond the woods," Violet told the lady. "He's very sick, so Mama sent us off with soup and cookies to help him feel better. Because cookies are good medicine—that's what Mama says."

"What sweet children," the lady said. "I'll be heading that way myself."

"Thinking there was a shortcut, the children followed the lady and her puppy off the elevator and into the deep, dark woods."

"Clouds covered the moon. The little girl and her brother were not in the woods anymore," Violet said. "They stepped inside a damp, dingy cave."

"We're not lost, Peter, I promise."

"Bats blinked from the ceiling.

Creepy, crackly spiders

scuttled across the floor."

"The little girl spied moonlight up ahead."

"The children plunged through brush and brambles until at last they emerged . . .

. . . right back on the path."

"See, Peter?
I told you we
weren't lost."

"Owls hooted,
coyotes barked,
and on a mountain in the distance
a wolf howled,"

Violet said.

"Don't worry, Peter. There are no real
wolves in apartment buildings."

WOOF!

"No wolves,
but there *are*
trolls."

"They were nearly at
Papa Jean-Louis's and that's
the end of the story!" Violet said.

However, deep in the shadows, a shaggy
something breathed. Violet held Peter's tiny
hand and walked just a little faster.

312

"I promise, Peter,
there are no wolves
in apartment buildings."

But something growled
in the shadows.

Violet ran, her wagon bumping
and rolling behind her.

"There are
no wolves, Peter!
No wolves,
no wolves!"

She kept on running with a slobbery, panting creature right behind them until . . .

Papa Jean-Louis's doormat welcomed Violet and Peter just ahead.

"We made it,"
Violet said.

On the couch sat Papa Jean-Louis with a cozy
blanket tucked up under his chin and a fuzzy
winter scarf wrapped all around his head.

"Papa Jean-Louis, we brought you
soup and cookies," Violet said.
Papa Jean-Louis didn't say a word.

Violet peered at Papa Jean-Louis.

"Why, Papa Jean-Louis,
your **eyes**
are so
big."

Violet stepped closer.

"Your
ears
are so . . .
hairy."

"And
your
teeth..."

Violet leaned in.

Papa Jean-Louis leaped forward. His scarf flew from his head. A furry tail whipped out from under the blanket.

"You're **not** Papa Jean-Louis.

You're a . . ."

"Wolf!"
Violet cried.

OOOF!

SNAP !

The wolf gobbled up a cookie in one slobbery bite. Violet grabbed Peter. But where was Papa Jean-Louis?

"Papa Jean-Louis, please don't be eaten!"

Violet raced down the hall.

The wolf bounded past her . . .

. . . leaped onto Papa Jean-Louis's bed,
opened a mouth full of razor-sharp teeth . . .

. . . and *slluuuurrrrrrped* Papa Jean-
Louis on the nose.
   "Look, Rosalie! What good children to
bring old Papa and Samson supper in bed."
Papa Jean-Louis smiled.

"WOOF!" said Peter.

"See, Peter?" Violet said, "I told you there are no wolves in apartment buildings. Just woofs!"

Violet decided her story needed a happy ending.
"Papa Jean-Louis and his daughter, Rosalie, shared
the soup with the children," said Violet. "But Samson,
who was not a wolf, did not share the cookies.

The end."